The Mystery of the
Silly Goose

THREE COUSINS DETECTIVE CLUB®

The Mystery of the Silly Goose

Elspeth Campbell Murphy
Illustrated by Joe Nordstrom

BETHANY HOUSE PUBLISHERS
MINNEAPOLIS, MINNESOTA 55438

The Mystery of the Silly Goose
Copyright © 1996
Elspeth Campbell Murphy

Cover and story illustrations by Joe Nordstrom

THREE COUSINS DETECTIVE CLUB® is a registered
trademark of Elspeth Campbell Murphy.

Scripture quotation is from the International Children's Bible.

Published by Bethany House Publishers
A Ministry of Bethany Fellowship, Inc.
11300 Hampshire Avenue South
Minneapolis, Minnesota 55438

Printed in the United States of America.

Library of Congress Cataloging-in-Publication Data

CIP applied for.

ELSPETH CAMPBELL MURPHY has been a familiar name in Christian publishing for over fifteen years, with more than seventy-five books to her credit and sales reaching five million worldwide. She is the author of the best-selling series *David and I Talk to God* and *The Kids From Apple Street Church*, as well as the 1990 Gold Medallion winner *Do You See Me, God?* A graduate of Trinity College and Moody Bible Institute, Elspeth and her husband, Mike, make their home in Chicago, where she writes full time.

Contents

It takes wisdom to have a good family.
It takes understanding to make it strong.
It takes knowledge to fill a home
with rare and beautiful treasures.

Proverbs 24:3–4

1

Lyddie

"So—you're, like, *finally back!*"

Timothy Dawson looked out of the car window and groaned. Vacation had been fun. Even educational. But now it was over. He was tired and cranky from the trip home. And the last thing he wanted to see standing in his driveway was his neighbor, Lyddie Jones.

Lyddie was thirteen, three years older than Timothy and his cousins Sarah-Jane Cooper and Titus McKay. She seemed to think that made her a grown-up compared to them. Most of the time she just ignored them.

But now she stood glaring in at them, hands on hips, foot tapping impatiently. "So—are you, like, going to get out of the car sometime today, or what?"

"What's *her* problem?" muttered Titus. "What does *she* care if we're back or not?"

"Good question," said Timothy. He made no move to get out of the car with his parents and his little sister, Priscilla. He was getting curious about what Lyddie wanted. But there was no point in letting her know that.

Sarah-Jane whispered, "Lyddie always wears such cute outfits. But as a person, she's really annoying."

"That's where you're wrong, S-J," said Timothy. "As a person, Lyddie Jones goes way, *way* beyond annoying."

Well, he could be pretty annoying, too, when he put his mind to it.

Slowly, slowly Timothy opened the car door. Slowly, slowly he climbed out. Titus and Sarah-Jane crawled out after him.

Timothy stretched and smiled up at the trees and the sky.

Then he blinked at Lyddie as if he had just noticed her for the first time.

"Why, hello, Lydia. Did you come out to welcome us home? That was very nice of you."

"Listen, you little twerp. I need your help with something. And I don't want any trouble out of you. Now, get over here." She turned to Titus and Sarah-Jane. "You, too."

"Well, since you asked us so nicely . . ." said Titus.

"Cute socks!" exclaimed Sarah-Jane.

"Thanks!" said Lyddie. "My grandma got them for me at the mall. Now, listen up. Something totally odd has been going on around here."

2

Lyddie's News

By now Timothy was wildly curious. But he just yawned and said, "Cut it out, Lyddie. You know that nothing ever happens around here."

This was not exactly true.

The three cousins had a detective club. And they had solved some mysteries in Timothy's neighborhood before. Titus and Sarah-Jane glanced at Timothy in surprise. But they didn't say anything. They knew when he was up to something.

The idea that there might be another mystery to solve made Timothy forget all about being tired and cranky. But he knew that if he looked too interested, Lyddie would clam up and not tell them anything.

She was like that.

As it was, Lyddie looked ready to explode. "Ha! That shows how much *you* know! It just so happens that something BIG has been going on around here. Now, do you want to hear about it or not?"

Titus glanced at his watch. "Sure. I have some time to kill before my parents come to pick me up."

Sarah-Jane shrugged. "Same here."

"Fire away," said Timothy.

"Well!" said Lyddie. She took a deep breath and paused dramatically. "There has been, like, this rash of burglaries in the neighborhood."

"Burglaries!" squeaked Timothy, forgetting to look bored. "You mean someone has been breaking into houses?" He looked toward his own house in alarm.

"No, silly!" said Lyddie. "The thieves didn't have to break into any houses."

"Why not?" asked Titus. "You mean they were stealing cars right out of the garages?"

"No!" said Lyddie. "Nothing was stolen out of any garages. Will you forget about houses and garages? I'm talking about thieves taking stuff right out of people's yards!"

"What do you mean?" asked Sarah-Jane. "Did some people forget to put their bikes or lawn mowers away and they got stolen?"

"No!" wailed Lyddie. "No, no, no, no! What is the matter with you people? Would you just listen for two seconds? I am trying to tell you something serious. And all you do is interrupt me with ridiculous questions!"

Timothy shrugged. They couldn't help asking questions. It was what detectives did. "Just tell us what's missing," he said.

"Lawn ornaments!" said Lyddie.

3

Lawn Ornaments

"*L*awn ornaments," repeated Timothy. "You mean—what? Flamingoes? Frogs? Stuff like that?"

"Well, duh!" said Lyddie.

Sarah-Jane sighed and rolled her eyes.

Titus looked at his watch again.

Timothy smiled pleasantly. "It's always so good to chat with you, Lydia. I believe you wanted our help with something. But I'm afraid we're just too dumb. Have a nice day."

"All right, all right, all right," snapped Lyddie. "Just be quiet and listen. All up and down the block people have had their lawn ornaments stolen. It happened last night, I guess. When people got up this morning, the stuff was gone."

15

"I see," said Timothy in his best detective voice. "Did anyone call the police?"

"The police!" exclaimed Lyddie as if this were a new idea to her. "Oh, right. I'm so sure people are going to report *lawn ornaments!*"

"You said this was big," replied Timothy.

"Not *that* big," snorted Lyddie.

Timothy narrowed his eyes thoughtfully and looked at Lyddie. She was not the type to worry about other people's flamingoes.

"So what's all this to you?" he asked. "Your family doesn't even have a lawn ornament."

Lyddie tossed her head. "Ha! That shows

how much *you* know. It just so happens that while you were on vacation, my grandmother came to live with us. And it just so happens that she brought some of her stuff with her. And it just so happens that one of the things was a lawn ornament. So there."

"What was it?" asked Sarah-Jane.

"What was *what*?" asked Lyddie as if they had gotten way off the subject.

"What was your grandmother's ornament?"

Lyddie hesitated. "A goose, all right? It was a goose. She was wearing a funny little hat. And she had these, like, little duckling-things following along behind her."

"Goslings," said Titus.

Lyddie gave him a long, cool stare. *"What?"*

"Goslings," repeated Titus. "Baby geese are called goslings. Baby ducks are called ducklings. If we're talking about a goose, I doubt very much she had ducklings with her."

Lyddie made a move as if to strangle him.

Titus hopped back and said brightly, "So. How can we help you?"

4

The T.C.D.C.

*F*or once Lyddie seemed at a loss for words. Finally she said, "OK, look. I know you guys do all that detective stuff. I want you to come talk to my grandma. Tell her you'll try to find out what happened to the goose. Maybe it will make her feel better to know that someone is looking for it."

"Why don't you look for the goose yourself?" asked Sarah-Jane reasonably.

"Me!?" cried Lyddie. "I have stuff to do."

"Like what?" asked Timothy. "Going to the mall with your snotty friends?"

Lyddie stood up straighter and looked down at him. "I am not even going to dignify that remark with an answer. But for your information, buster, you're not the only one who goes on vacation, you know. It just so happens that two of my best and coolest friends are both getting back today. So I *have* to see them."

"In other words," said Titus, "you want to send someone else off on a 'wild goose chase.' "

"Oh, that is so not-funny," snapped Lyddie. "So are you going to help my grandmother, or what?"

The cousins looked at one another and shrugged.

"Sure, why not?" said Timothy.

Lyddie turned and led the way with the three cousins trotting along behind her to keep up. It seemed to Timothy that they must look like a mother goose with her goslings. But he decided not to say so. He had given Lyddie a hard enough time for one day—so far.

Lyddie's grandmother was sitting in a lawn chair in the yard. Timothy didn't think she seemed all that old. But she looked tired—as if maybe she had been sick for a while. Still, when she looked up at them, her smile was bright and her eyes were twinkly.

Lyddie went over and hugged her gently.

"Grandma, here are those detective kids I was telling you about. My neighbor and his cousins. Please, *please* don't feel so bad about the goose! They're going to see if they can find it, OK?"

Timothy couldn't believe his ears. He had never heard Lyddie speak so nicely to anyone. Not even to her snotty friends.

Lyddie's grandmother smiled up at the cousins. "I'm Lydia Hamilton," she said. "And you are Timothy, Titus, and Sarah-Jane?"

"Yes, ma'am," said Timothy politely. "The T.C.D.C. is at your service."

"What's a 'teesy-deesy'?" asked Mrs. Hamilton.

"It's letters," explained Sarah-Jane. "Capital T. Capital C. Capital D. Capital C. It stands for the Three Cousins Detective Club."

"Well, I hope you can help me," said Lyddie's grandmother. "And the other people who lost ornaments, too. It seems strange, all of it happening at once like that, doesn't it? What in the world would someone want with all those ornaments?"

"Maybe it was just some kind of prank,"

suggested Titus. "A bad practical joke."

"Perhaps so," said Mrs. Hamilton. "But I'm afraid it's not very funny to the people who lost things. My silly little goose wasn't valuable, of course. But someone very precious gave her to me. So it had a great deal of sentimental value. I've had her a long time. And with her in the yard, I felt right at home here. I appreciate your looking into this for me. But I'm afraid I don't hold out much hope of seeing my silly goose again."

Lyddie opened her mouth as if to say something. But just then a car pulled up, and a horn honked.

"There's my ride," she said. "Gotta go! Bye, Grandma!"

The cousins stood looking after her as she flew off down the sidewalk.

5

Little Red Wagon

"So," said Sarah-Jane when the three cousins were back at Timothy's house. "Where do we start?"

"It's a long shot," said Timothy. "But we could talk to other people who lost things. Maybe somebody knows something. Let's just go up and down the block. I think I'll be able to tell where things are missing."

It *was* a long shot, but a lot of detective work was just "pounding the pavement." Going door to door. Talking to people. So Timothy felt pretty cheerful when he went off to tell his parents what he and his cousins were up to.

When he came back, he was pulling a little red wagon. It had been his ever since he was a baby. Now it mostly belonged to his sister, Priscilla, who was still a toddler.

"What's the wagon for, Tim?" asked Titus.

"You never know," said Timothy. "If we get lucky and find the goose and her goslings, we'll need a way to bring them back."

"Good thinking," said Titus.

Unfortunately, Priscilla had spotted them. "Wide! Wide! Wide!" she screamed.

"I think she wants to go for a ride in the wagon," said Sarah-Jane, who understood baby talk pretty well.

"I think I'd better take her," sighed Timothy, who understood Priscilla pretty well. "Once she gets an idea in her head, there's no reasoning with her." He called to Priscilla, "OK, Sib, come on. We don't have all day."

Timothy's mother smiled gratefully at them. Priscilla trotted over with her blankie and a pillow from the couch.

"Make yourself comfortable, Cuz," Titus told her with a laugh.

Priscilla nodded happily. "O-tay."

Timothy, Titus, and Sarah-Jane were eager to get started.

But Priscilla spotted a baby buggy on the

front walk of a nearby house and pointed at it.

"See baby!" She always loved to look at babies who were smaller than she was.

Timothy said, "We don't have time, Sib. We're asking people about lost lawn ornaments. This is the Baileys' house. They never had a lawn ornament. Besides, the baby wouldn't be out in the buggy all by himself."

"SEE BABY!"

Sarah-Jane said, "You guys wait here. I'll take her to look in the buggy. It's the only way she'll believe us."

Sarah-Jane snatched Priscilla out of the wagon and hurried up the walk.

Timothy and Titus saw Sarah-Jane lean over and look in the buggy.

Then they heard her scream.

6

One Ugly Baby

*T*imothy and Titus rushed up the walk just as Mrs. Bailey rushed out the front door.

"What happened?! What's wrong?!" they all asked at once.

Sarah-Jane set Priscilla down and tried to catch her breath. "I'm sorry. I didn't expect to see . . . Well, certainly not . . . that—*thing*!"

Titus looked in the buggy and jumped back. "Whoa! That is one ugly baby!"

Mrs. Bailey looked in the buggy and shrieked, "Good grief! What *is* that?"

Timothy looked in the buggy and burst out laughing. "It's a gnome!" he said.

"A *what*?" cried Sarah-Jane.

"A gnome," repeated Timothy. "You know. It's a kind of dwarf from a fairy tale."

"Oh," said Sarah-Jane. But she still sounded confused.

She helped Timothy to haul the brightly painted statue out of the buggy and set it on the sidewalk. It really did look like something from *Snow White*. It was just about the same size as Priscilla. Priscilla laughed in delight and threw her arms around it.

"Mine baby!"

"No, it isn't," said Timothy sternly. "It belongs to the Murrays. They live across the

street from us. We have to take it back to them."

To the others he explained, "I know about this being a gnome because the Murrays told me about it. They brought it back all the way from England."

Titus eyed the gnome doubtfully. "Why?"

"To decorate their yard," answered Timothy. "This is called a garden gnome. In other words—a *lawn ornament.*"

"Oh!" cried Titus and Sarah-Jane together.

Mrs. Bailey said, "I heard about those ornaments being stolen. But how in the world did this gnome-thing end up in my baby buggy?"

The cousins looked at one another.

That was a good question.

7

Funny Weird

Mrs. Bailey was only too glad to have the cousins take the garden gnome back where it belonged. Her baby was inside napping, so she couldn't go to the Murrays' herself.

Priscilla liked the gnome so much, she seemed to have forgotten all about not seeing the real baby.

Timothy helped her climb back into the wagon. Then he and Titus lifted the gnome in after her.

"Scooch over, Sib. You've got company."

"Mine baby."

Timothy sighed. "No, it isn't. And didn't we just have this conversation?"

It was so hard to get through to Priscilla sometimes. But then again, it was because she *had* to see the baby that they had found the gnome in the first place. And that got Timothy thinking.

"You know what's funny?" he said to Titus and Sarah-Jane as they walked along.

"Funny ha-ha? Or funny weird?" asked Titus.

"Funny weird," replied Timothy.

"What's funny weird?" asked Sarah-Jane.

"How we found that lawn ornament. I mean, it was hidden in such an easy place even a baby could find it. In fact, a baby *did* find it."

Priscilla was not paying attention to this. She was chattering away to the gnome in baby talk that not even Sarah-Jane could understand. From time to time she gave his nose a friendly tug or poked her finger in his eye. Timothy had to admit that the gnome was so ugly it was cute.

"I see what you mean about the hiding place, Tim," said Titus slowly. "Even if Priscilla hadn't found the gnome, Mrs. Bailey's baby would have. I mean, as soon as Mrs. Bailey went to put her baby in the buggy . . ."

" . . . the stolen lawn ornament would be found," finished Sarah-Jane.

"Right," said Timothy. "If you wanted to hide something so it *wouldn't* be found . . ."

" . . . then the baby buggy was not a good hiding place," finished Sarah-Jane.

They were quiet for a moment, thinking about this.

Finally Titus said, "But that doesn't make sense. Why go to all the trouble of hiding something if you know it won't stay hidden?"

"None of this makes sense," said Timothy. "Why go to the trouble of stealing the lawn ornaments at all? Obviously, the thieves didn't keep the Murrays' garden gnome for themselves."

"Or sell it to someone else," added Sarah-Jane.

Titus shook his head. "All I can think of is that it's some kind of practical joke. A lawn ornament is taken. But not so that it will be gone for good. Only so that it will be gone for a little while."

"It's still a mean thing to do," said Sarah-Jane. "How are people supposed to know that they'll get their lawn ornaments back?"

"We don't even know if they will," said

Timothy. "We found only one so far."

"And it's not the goose," said Titus.

"That's right," agreed Sarah-Jane. "It's not the goose."

8

The Fwoggie

*T*imothy knew that the Murrays would be glad to get their funny little gnome back.

He also knew that a certain funny little person wouldn't want to give it back.

He was right, of course.

Priscilla howled when he lifted the gnome out of the wagon.

But she stopped howling when she saw what Mr. Murray was holding.

"Waz dat?" she asked, pointing at it.

Sarah-Jane explained. "It's a frog. It's for decorating the yard. It's a nice froggie, isn't it?"

"Mine fwoggie!"

Timothy groaned. "Here we go again. It isn't yours, Sib. It belongs to Mr. Murray."

"Well, actually, it doesn't," said Mr. Murray. "I just found it a couple of minutes ago. I went to sit down on my porch swing. Then I felt something hard and lumpy behind the cushion."

Titus exclaimed, "Weirder and weirder! First the gnome in the baby buggy. And now the frog on the swing. It's almost as if the thieves *wanted* the things to be found."

"It's just crazy," agreed Mr. Murray. "What in the world is going on around here?"

"That's what we'd like to find out," said Timothy. He explained about Lyddie wanting them to look for her grandmother's goose and goslings.

"I can't imagine why anyone would want to steal that goose," said Mr. Murray. He sighed and shook his head. "It's amazing what some people will put in their yards, isn't it?"

The cousins couldn't help glancing at the gnome. But they were too polite to say anything.

"See fwoggie!" demanded Priscilla.

"Oh, right," said Timothy, suddenly remembering the other missing ornaments. He said to Mr. Murray, "We'll take the frog back where it belongs if you'd like."

"That's very nice of you," said Mr. Murray. "I think it belongs to the Changs up the block."

Timothy set the frog in the wagon. Priscilla smiled at it and thumped it on the head. Timothy realized she would probably howl when they gave the frog back to the Changs. But he would cross that bridge when he came to it. Maybe he should talk to his parents about getting an ornament for their own yard. Priscilla seemed to like them so much. And not even she could break one.

Mr. Murray helped Timothy make a list of all the ornaments that had been taken.

Then the cousins started off again. They were all quiet, thinking things over. They loved detective work. But this was getting frustrating. What did it all mean?

9

Something Silly

At least one thing worked out well. Priscilla didn't howl when they gave the frog back to the Changs. That's because the motion of the wagon had rocked her to sleep.

"What do you want to do next, Tim?" whispered Titus.

"Let's take Priscilla home," Timothy whispered back. "Then we can work on this list."

"Good idea," whispered Sarah-Jane.

The cousins practically tiptoed all the way back to Timothy's house.

Timothy went inside to ask his mother to come get Priscilla.

Then he and Sarah-Jane and Titus studied the list.

The Murrays had lost a garden gnome.

✓ Murrays - garden gnome

✓ Changs - frog

(Hamilton - goose, goslings)

Greens - rabbit

Johnsons - flamingo

Taylors - fawn

Timothy dug a pencil out of his pocket. He put a check mark beside that one, because the gnome had been found.

The Changs had lost a frog. Timothy put a check mark by that one, too.

Mrs. Hamilton, Lyddie's grandmother, had lost a goose and goslings. Timothy circled that one since it was what Lyddie had sort of "hired" them to find.

The Greens had lost a rabbit.

The Johnsons had lost a flamingo.

The Taylors had lost part of a deer family.

Not the buck—the father. Not the doe—the mother. Just the fawn—the baby.

Sarah-Jane said, "Why do you think they took just the baby deer? Because it was the cutest?"

"Probably because it was the smallest," said Titus. "Lawn ornaments are heavier than they look."

"That's true," agreed Sarah-Jane. "The big mother and father deer would be kind of heavy and bulky to carry. I wonder if that means there was only one thief? Lyddie said 'thieves,' but who knows?"

Timothy and Titus agreed that this was a good point.

"Except . . ." Sarah-Jane continued. "Why would you do anything so silly all by yourself? I mean, usually when someone does something silly, it's because a whole bunch of people are doing that silly thing together. And stealing lawn ornaments and hiding them in silly places is about as silly as you can get. It's just plain—"

"Silly?" guessed Titus. "You're right, S-J. It *is* just plain silly. Unless . . . there's a logical explanation that we haven't figured out yet."

They walked along, thinking about this when suddenly Sarah-Jane stopped and pointed to the edge of some bushes.

She said softly, "Oh, look! Look! It's a little bunny rabbit!"

They froze in place.

The rabbit was frozen, too, the way rabbits are when they're frightened.

"Let's see how close we can get," said Timothy, whispering. They seemed to be whispering a lot lately.

"OK. But don't scare him," whispered Sarah-Jane.

Very, very carefully they moved forward.

The rabbit didn't hop away.

They crept a little closer, hardly daring to breathe.

It looked as if the rabbit was holding his breath, too. He sat so still, not even quivering.

"I wonder if he'd let us touch him?" murmured Titus.

Timothy murmured back, "You can try it. But he's sure to hop away then."

But the rabbit didn't hop away when Titus touched him.

He didn't even try to wiggle free when Titus picked him up.

That's because he was made of plaster.

10

Pounding the Pavement

"*H*e's very real looking," said Sarah-Jane, sounding rather annoyed with the rabbit for fooling them.

Titus laughed. "So is his little friend."

"What little friend?" asked Timothy.

Titus reached a bit farther into the bushes and pulled out . . . a baby deer!

Timothy reached into his pocket and pulled out the list and a pencil. He put a check mark by the rabbit and a check mark by the fawn.

"The rabbit goes back to the Greens," he said. "And the fawn goes back to the Taylors."

The cousins put the lawn ornament animals in the wagon and started off again. Pounding the pavement. Keeping their eyes open for a flamingo and a goose.

A lot of detective work was just staying alert and noticing things.

Timothy was an artist, as well as a detective. As an artist, he always noticed the colors and shapes of things. As a detective, he always noticed when something seemed odd or out of place.

And that's how they found the Johnsons' flamingo.

Timothy happened to notice a spot of bright pink plastic among the dark green leaves of a big nearby tree.

The flamingo was caught on one of the lower branches but too high to reach. It looked as if someone had just tossed it up there.

Titus was the expert at climbing trees. So Timothy and Sarah-Jane gave him a boost, and Titus scrambled up after the flamingo.

He handed it down to Sarah-Jane as Timothy checked the flamingo off the list.

"Well, that just about does it," Timothy said when Titus had swung himself back down. "All we have to do now is take these things back. Then we'll find the goose and her goslings. And we can wrap this case up."

They took the lawn ornaments back where they belonged. The owners were all delighted, of course.

But the cousins didn't get to wrap the case up.

That was because they couldn't find the goose.

11

Wild Goose Chase

"*T*his is ridiculous," said Titus. "All the other stuff practically jumped out at us. So why can't we find the goose?"

The three cousins sat glumly on the front porch of Timothy's house and thought about this. After finding the other ornaments, they thought finding the goose would be a cinch.

It wasn't.

They had gone back up the block and down again. They had talked to anyone who might know something.

But there was no sign anywhere of the goose and her goslings.

Sarah-Jane said, "It's like Ti said before. This is a 'wild goose chase.' We started off looking for the goose. And we found everything *except* the goose. Lyddie is not going to be too happy about this! But if Lyddie cares so much about her grandmother's feelings, she should be here helping us. Not off with her friends. I mean, sure—it's OK to be with your friends. But you have to help your family when they need you. Why should we have to do all the work? It's Lyddie's grandmother."

"Lyddie!" snorted Timothy. "When she gets back—*if* she ever gets back—I'm going to tell her to find the goose herself. *I quit!* This wild goose chase is just too annoying."

Titus said, "Speaking of annoying . . ."

A car had just pulled up next door. Out came Lyddie and her two 'best and coolest' friends.

"Let's get this over with," said Timothy. "Lyddie will probably throw a fit. But that's just too bad."

The cousins got up and went over to Lyddie's house.

Timothy was glad Lyddie's grandmother wasn't outside. He didn't want to have to tell her that they couldn't find the goose. But he *did* want to tell *Lyddie* that the T.C.D.C. was off the case.

12

Aliens on the Sidewalk

*L*yddie sat on her front porch with her friends. They were looking over all the cute little stuff they had bought at the mall.

When she saw the cousins, she jumped back in horror as if aliens had just landed on her front sidewalk.

"What do you want?" she demanded.

"We come in peace, Lydia," said Timothy. "We just need to talk to you for a minute."

"Me!?" cried Lyddie. "What do you want to talk to me for?"

"Lyddie!" gasped one of her friends. "You don't, like, actually *know* them, do you? I mean, they're just little kids!"

"They live next door," said Lyddie apologetically. She pointed at Timothy. "At least he does. But I've never actually, like, *talked* to them before."

The cousins looked at one another. Just when you thought things couldn't get any weirder . . .

Sarah-Jane spoke slowly and clearly, the way she did to Priscilla. "Lyddie. We need to talk to you. It's about the lawn ornaments that—"

"Lawn ornaments!" cried Lyddie's other friend. "Oh, gross! I totally hate those things. They are, like, so weird. I mean, we talked about that before, remember? How, like, if our parents ever got one of those things we would just *die* of embarrassment and have to move away. Remember?"

"I remember," said Lyddie.

"How could you move away if you were dead?" asked Titus in his most reasonable tone of voice.

"Lyddie!" wailed her two friends together. *"Do* something! Make them go away."

Lyddie gave a heavy sigh and stood up. "Let me talk to them," she said. "It's the only way they'll leave us alone."

She hopped off the porch and herded the

cousins out of her yard and over to Timothy's.

When they were out of earshot of her friends, Lyddie got down to business.

"OK. Did you do what I wanted?"

Titus said, "Wait a minute. Does this mean that you actually *have* talked to us before?"

"Never mind that," said Lyddie briskly. "I just don't want to be embarrassed in front of my friends, that's all. So—what did you find?"

"We found the lawn ornaments," began Timothy.

"All of them?" asked Lyddie.

"All except the goose and goslings," said Timothy.

The cousins stepped back, expecting an explosion.

But Lyddie just nodded. "So all the neighbors got their stuff back?"

"All except your grandmother," said Timothy.

Lyddie shook her head sadly. "I guess that's just the way it is when there's a rash of burglaries. Some people get their stuff back, and some people don't."

"We feel so sorry for your grandmother," Sarah-Jane began. "If you want us to—"

But Lyddie just patted her shoulder like an understanding teacher. "I'm sure you did your best, and that's all that matters. I'll tell my grandmother you tried. She'll appreciate that. But you don't have to bother looking for the goose anymore."

And with that she turned and hurried back to her friends.

The cousins stood staring after her.

"Well, I guess that's that," said Titus.

"We didn't even have to tell her that we were quitting," said Sarah-Jane.

"Are you kidding?" said Timothy. "We're going to find that goose if it's the last thing we do."

13

Priscilla's Duckie

Sarah-Jane and Titus turned to Timothy in surprise. But before they could ask him anything, Timothy's mother called to the cousins from the backyard.

The backyard was fenced in so that Priscilla couldn't get out. But she still needed watching.

Timothy had a feeling he knew what was coming.

He was right.

Priscilla was up from her nap and playing in her sandbox.

Their mother said, "Priscilla should be OK for a while. But I have all the unpacking to do. I need you to watch her for me. OK?"

Timothy was about to protest that he had

to keep looking for Mrs. Hamilton's goose. But the truth was, he had no idea where to look next. It wouldn't hurt just to sit and think for a while. So he said, "I'm in charge here, Sib. No pouring sand in your ears!"

Priscilla nodded happily. "O-tay! Mine duckie!"

Timothy's mother went inside. And Timothy, Titus, and Sarah-Jane each grabbed a swing on the gym set. They swung gently back and forth, not getting off the ground, because they wanted to talk.

Sarah-Jane said, "Why do you want to keep looking for the goose, Tim? Lyddie said just to forget about finding it."

"That's exactly *why* I want to find it," replied Timothy. "If you ask me, Lyddie has been acting pretty strange."

"How can you tell?" asked Titus. "I mean, if Lyddie acted like a normal person, *that* would be strange—for her."

"Mine duckie," said Priscilla.

"That's right, sweetie," Sarah-Jane called to her. "You just keep playing like a good girl. We're talking here. But we can still watch you."

"Mine duckie."

"That's right."

Titus said, "Let's just say that Lyddie *is* acting strange—even for her. That still doesn't tell us where the goose is. Or why we could find everything except that."

Sarah-Jane said, "When you think about it, it's kind of lucky for Lyddie that we *couldn't* find the goose. Her friends think lawn ornaments are gross and weird. Lyddie would die of embarrassment if they knew about her grandmother's goose. But they don't know. They were both on vacation when Lyddie's grandmother moved in. And the goose had been stolen before they got back."

"And now we can't find it," said Titus. "Lucky Lyddie."

Timothy didn't say anything. An idea was beginning to take shape in his mind. But he didn't quite have it yet.

"Saywah-Zane! Tum see duckie?"

"I'd better check on her," said Sarah-Jane. She got off the swing and went over to Priscilla in the sandbox.

Suddenly she called, "Hey, you guys! Come here! Quick!"

Timothy and Titus rushed over.

Sarah-Jane pointed to the thing Priscilla was holding. She said, "Does that look like a duckie to you?"

"Nope," said Titus. "The bill is all wrong."

"All wrong for a duckling," said Timothy. "But that's a gosling."

14

The Duckie's Mommy

*T*he three cousins took a deep breath all at the same time. This was not going to be easy.

Sarah-Jane knelt down and said, "Priscilla? Listen, sweetie. Can you tell Sarah-Jane where you found the duckie?"

"Mine duckie."

"Yes, it's a nice duckie, isn't it? Where did you get it?"

"Mine duckie."

Sarah-Jane tried again. "We need to find the duckie's mommy, Priscilla."

Titus muttered. " 'The duckie's mommy'? Oh, please!"

Sarah-Jane smiled sweetly. "Somebody needs to be quiet, doesn't he? Now, Priscilla. You're a good helper. First you found the gnome. Then you found the duckie. Now, can you help us find the duckie's mommy? She must be somewhere near the duckie. So tell us where you found the duckie."

The cousins held their breath. With one chubby little hand Priscilla hugged the gosling close. With the other she pointed to the ground in front of a big box by the back of the house. The box was used for holding firewood in the winter. It would be empty now. Unless . . .

Timothy, Titus, and Sarah-Jane rushed to the box and lifted the lid.

The wild goose chase was over.

Inside were the goose and her goslings.

They lined up the goose and her goslings all in a row. It was easy to see why Lyddie would be embarrassed. Sure, the goose was cute—but in a silly-looking way. It was hard to imagine who would want something like that in the yard.

"PWITTY CHICKEN! MINE CHICKEN!"

Priscilla. That's who.

The cousins looked at one another.

This was not going to be easy.

Timothy said, "It's a goose, Sib. And the goose wants to go for a ride. Let's put the goose and her babies in the wagon."

"O-tay."

Titus pointed at the firewood box.

"You know what I think of that hiding place? EX-cellent."

"Neat-O," agreed Timothy. "Because if the thief hadn't dropped one of the goslings, we would never have thought of looking there."

Sarah-Jane added, "That hiding place was so cool. Because the goose wouldn't even have been found until it was time to load up the box for winter!"

"Right," said Timothy. "And then it would be time to put the goose away in the garage or the basement."

The idea that had been fuzzy at the back of his mind suddenly became clear. And he told his cousins about it.

Sarah-Jane said, "You mean the thief is—?! But what kind of person would steal from her own grandmother?"

"I rest my case," said Timothy.

15

Home for a Goose

*L*yddie's friends had gone by the time the cousins pulled the wagon around to the front of Lydia's house. Priscilla trotted along behind them.

Timothy said in a sweet, singsongy voice, "Oh, Lyd-i-a! We have a sur-prise for you!"

Lyddie gasped when she saw the goose. Then she tried to smile. "Why, why—that's wonderful. Where did you find it?"

"Where do you think we found it?" asked Timothy. "Right where you hid it."

"Me!?" cried Lyddie. "I don't know what you're talking about!"

"Oh, give it up, Lyddie," said Timothy. "You didn't want your snotty friends to see your grandmother's goose in your yard. So you hid it. And then you made it look like it was just one of a lot of other burglaries. But you didn't want to get in serious trouble. So you brought us in on the case. That's because you knew we would find the other stuff and get it back where it belonged. But you *didn't* want us to find the goose. You just said you did so that no one would suspect that you were the one who took it in the first place."

Titus said, "It was all pretty smart in a sneaky sort of way. You could have been a first-rate detective, Lyddie. If only you hadn't chosen a life of crime."

Lyddie sank down on the porch and put her head in her hands. "Oh, why doesn't the ground just open and swallow me up?"

Timothy said cheerfully, "Sounds like a plan to me."

"You don't understand!" wailed Lyddie. "I didn't know what else to do. I had to get rid of that goose. But I didn't want to hurt my grandmother's feelings about it. She has such good taste in some things. Like socks and stuff. But that goose! It's so silly looking!"

They were all suddenly aware of the sound of someone laughing.

It was Lyddie's grandmother, standing in the doorway.

She came out and sat down beside Lyddie and put her arms around her.

"Oh, sweetie!" she said. "Don't you remember who gave me that goose? That very precious person?"

Lyddie shook her head.

"It was you!"

"Me!?"

"Yes, I thought you knew that. You were

only four years old. And you picked out the goose for my birthday present. And no one could talk you out of it. You gave me that goose. And that is why it is one of my dearest treasures. But believe me, I understand how hard it is to have your friends laugh at you. So we'll have to think of something."

Priscilla, who had been quiet all this time, patted the goose on the head. She said proudly, "Pwitty chicken. Mine chicken."

"Why, now, there's an idea!" exclaimed Mrs. Hamilton. "I couldn't bear to part with my silly goose forever. But I could certainly *lend* her to someone. Especially if the goose went to a place where I could still see her."

Lyddie caught on first. A slow smile crept across her face. "You mean—put the goose in Timothy's yard?"

"No!" wailed Timothy before he could stop himself.

"It wouldn't have to be the *front* yard," said Lyddie's grandmother.

"That's right," said Sarah-Jane. "If you put it back by the sandbox, it would just look like one of Priscilla's toys."

"Mine chicken."

Timothy knew when he was licked. "Let me ask my parents," he said.

Lyddie's grandmother said firmly to Lyddie, "And as for you, young lady. You need to tell your parents what you've been up to. And you'll be doing some apologizing to the neighbors, I've no doubt."

Lyddie accepted this without complaint. At least she didn't have the goose in her yard.

Sarah-Jane's parents and Titus's parents arrived soon after that. And all three families went out for pizza.

Timothy's father said, "I'll tell you, vacations are fun. But it's always great to come back home."

"That's true," said Timothy. "Even though nothing ever happens around here."

The End

Series for Young Readers*
From Bethany House Publishers

★ ★ ★

BACKPACK MYSTERIES
by Mary Carpenter Reid

This excitement-filled mystery series follows the mishaps and adventures of Steff and Paulie Larson as they strive to help often-eccentric relatives crack their toughest cases.

★ ★ ★

THE CUL-DE-SAC KIDS
by Beverly Lewis

Each story in this lighthearted series features the hilarious antics and predicaments of nine endearing boys and girls who live on Blossom Hill Lane.

★ ★ ★

RUBY SLIPPERS SCHOOL
by Stacy Towle Morgan

Join the fun as home-schoolers Hope and Annie Brown visit fascinating countries and meet inspiring Christians from around the world!

★ ★ ★

THE THREE COUSINS DETECTIVE CLUB®
by Elspeth Campbell Murphy

Famous detective cousins Timothy, Titus, and Sarah-Jane learn compelling Scripture-based truths while finding—and solving—intriguing mysteries.

* (ages 7–10)